MONSTER By Mistake!

Gorgool's Pet

Adapted by **Paul Kropp**

Based on the screenplay by
Steve Wright

Graphics by **Studio 345**

WINDING
STAIR
PRESS

Monster By Mistake
Theme Song

Hi my name is Warren and I'm just
a kid like you,

Or I was until I found evil
Gorgool's magic Jewel.

Then he tricked me and I read
a spell, now every
time I sneeze,

Monster By
Mistake . .

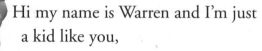

My sister Tracy tries the
Spell Book.

She never gets it right.

But Tracy doesn't ever give
up, 'cause you know one day
she might

Find the words that will
return me to my former width
and height.

I'm a Monster By Mista .... ah .... ah ...

I'm gonna tell you 'bout Johnny the
Ghost,

He's a wisecracking,
trumpet playing
friend.

He lives up in the
attic (shhh . . . Mom and
Dad don't know)

Johnny always has
a helping hand
to lend.

My secret Monster-iffic life always keeps
me on the run.

And I have a funny
feeling that the
story's just begun.

Everybody thinks it's
pretty awesome
I've become

A Monster By Mistake!

I'm a Monster By Mistake!

I'm a Monster By Mistake!

Monster by Mistake
Text © 2002 by Winding Stair
Graphics © 2002 by Monster by Mistake Enterprises Ltd.
Monster By Mistake Created by Mark Mayerson
Produced by CCI Entertainment Ltd. and Catapult Productions
Series Executive Producers: Arnie Zipursky and Kim Davidson

National Library of Canada Cataloging in Publication Data
Kropp, Paul, 1948–
    Gorgool's pet

(Monster by mistake ; 6)
Based on an episode of the television program, Monster by mistake.
ISBN 1-55366-215-6

I. Wright, Steve II. CCI Entertainment Ltd. III. Monster by mistake
(Television program) IV. Title. V. Series: Kropp, Paul, 1948– . Monster
by mistake ; 6.

PS8571.R772G67 2002   jC813'.54   C2002-900353-9
PZ7.K93Go 2002

Winding Stair Press
An imprint of Stewart House Publishing Inc.
290 North Queen Street, #210
Etobicoke, Ontario, M9C 5K4 Canada
1-866-574-6873

Executive Vice President and Publisher: Ken Proctor
Director of Publishing and Product Acquisition: Susan Jasper
Production Manager: Ruth Bradley-St-Cyr
Copy Editing: Martha Campbell
Text Design: Laura Brady
Cover Design: Darrin Laframboise

This book is available at special discounts for bulk purchases by
groups or organizations for sales promotions, premiums, fundraising
and educational purposes. For details, contact: Stewart House
Publishing Inc., Special Sales Department, 195 Allstate Parkway,
Markham, Ontario L3R 4T8. Toll free 1-866-474-3478.

1 2 3 4 5 6   07 06 05 04 03 02

Printed and bound in Canada

COLLECT THEM ALL

8 BOOKS SO FAR!

Contents

Chapter 1

Warren Patterson loved looking into his ant farm. Through the clear glass case, he could see everything the ants did. He watched them scurry through the dirt tunnels, hard at work. Like all ants, these were extremely busy. They carried food, dug new tunnels, and paraded up and down their sand hill.

Warren Patterson had even named his ants, at least the ones that seemed special. There were Rosie and Ethel, who seemed like sisters, and Herman, the largest of them all.

Setting down his ant-farm, Warren looked at his sister Tracy. "Aren't they wonderful?" he asked.

Tracy rolled her eyes. "I can't believe

you brought those bugs to our school picnic."

"They're not just bugs, Tracy. Ants are wonderful insects that work hard all day long. I bet if they were big, they'd be just like puppies. They'd probably enjoy this picnic!"

"Frankly, I'm glad they're small," Tracy told her brother. "I can't imagine playing fetch-the-stick with an ant. And you'd better be careful. Mr. Petrie said the ants shouldn't be left alone at this stage of their growth."

"I'm always careful, Tracy. Always," Warren replied. Then he picked up the farm again and stared through the glass walls.

*   *   *

If Warren had been really careful, he might have seen the evil Gorgool and his slack-jawed servant spying nearby. Gorgool was a small, ugly creature with a sharp horn who was trapped inside a clear ball. Since the ball made him helpless, he relied on his dimwitted servant for all of his needs.

"There it is," said Gorgool, looking down.

The servant looked puzzled. "The ant farm, master?"

"No, you fool! The girl's backpack!"

This pair of troublemakers weren't watching the Patterson kids. They needed what was in Tracy's backpack.

It all went back to when Gorgool first appeared in the town. Gorgool had got hold of the Jewel of Fenrath and the Book of Spells. These were the keys for him to get out of his sphere-shaped prison. Then Gorgool would be free to endanger everyone on Earth.

But just as the evil creature had been about to get loose, Warren and Tracy interrupted. Ever since then, the two kids carefully protected the jewel and the Book of Spells.

Still, Gorgool kept trying to get his hands on them. He and his servant made plan after plan in the basement of the ruined Amberson Mansion. He wasn't going to let the school picnic in Grover's Field spoil this plan.

"That girl always carries the book and jewel in that backpack," he told his servant. "If you can get them both, I'll finally be free of this wretched ball."

"Uh, yes, master," replied the servant, who had heard this so many times before.

A short way off, a whistle blew loudly. It was the Patterson kids' aunt Dolores. She was busy trying to round everyone up. "Attention!" she shouted. "The wheelbarrow race will begin shortly. Everyone should find a partner and a wheelbarrow – now!"

Tracy's friend Susan tugged on Tracy's sleeve, urging her to come choose a wheelbarrow for the race.

"I'm coming. I'm coming," Tracy told her friend.

Tracy took off with Susan, but left her backpack behind on the picnic blanket.

Fortunately, Warren was still nearby, looking at his ants. That kept Gorgool and the servant from making a move.

Suddenly, Warren heard a voice over his head. "Hey, kid. When's chow time?"

Warren looked up to see Johnny the Ghost. His ghostly friend had appeared out of nowhere and was eyeing the picnic basket on the blanket.

Warren quickly set his ant farm back down. "Johnny! There are too many people here! Someone is bound to see you."

"You worry too much," said Johnny, diving down inside the picnic basket. He popped back out of the top munching on a chicken leg. "I sure love fried chicken!"

Warren heard a voice call for him. It was his mother! Johnny quickly disappeared, but the chicken leg stayed floating in midair.

"Warren," said his mother, "the race teams are lining up ..." That was when

she noticed the drumstick floating behind her son.

"Yiiiii!" she screamed.

"What's wrong?" asked Warren.

Mrs. Patterson looked shaken. "Behind you! There's a chicken leg ... it's floating in the air!"

Johnny enjoyed teasing Mrs. Patterson like this. He kept on doing things that she couldn't explain. And Warren kept on covering up for him.

"Must be that new light oil they use for frying," said Warren grabbing the chicken leg as if there was nothing strange about it floating in the air. He put it back in the picnic basket.

When Mrs. Patterson took a few steps back, she accidentally knocked over the ant farm. Soon the ants came flooding out on the lawn.

Warren turned back to his mom, not noticing his tipped-over ant farm. "C'mon, mom, we're going to be late for the race!" he said, as the two of them raced to the starting line.

Chapter 2

Everyone had now left the picnic area and Tracy's backpack was unguarded. Gorgool's eyes lit up as he turned to his faithful servant.

"What are you waiting for? Get me the girl's backpack!"

The servant nearly saluted. "Yes, mighty Gorgool."

The servant, trying not to call attention to himself, had donned a pair of sunglasses and a big Western hat. On the servant's huge body, the outfit just made him stand out even more. Gorgool's servant crawled out from where he was hidden and crept over to the Patterson's blanket. Just as he was about to snatch the backpack, a voice shouted at him.

"Hey, you!"

It was Mr. Petrie, a teacher at Warren and Tracy's school.

The servant stood up quickly, trying to look innocent. "Uh, me?"

"Yes, you," said the energetic Mr. Petrie. "How'd you like to be my partner in the wheelbarrow race?"

The servant tried to think of something to say. His forehead wrinkled up with the effort. "Uh," he said.

"With a big guy like you, we'd win the trophy for sure!" exclaimed the teacher.

"Uh, I like to win, but ..." the servant scratched his head.

While they were talking, Tracy ran up. "Excuse me. I forgot my bag." She scooped up the backpack and ran off.

"So," said Mr. Petrie. "Are you with me?"

With a sigh, the servant followed the

teacher over to the race area. They selected
a wheelbarrow and lined up at the starting
line.

Aunt Dolores was in charge of the

event. "All right, contestants! Take your places!"

Mr. Petrie climbed into the wheelbarrow and sat down. The teacher could barely fit and his legs dangled over the front of the cart. The servant grabbed the

wheelbarrow by the handles. For this race their opponents were Tracy and Susan, Warren and his friend Connor, Mrs. Patterson and another teacher, and two other children.

"On your mark!" called Dolores. "Get set!" All the wheelbarrow pushers got ready to run. "Go!" Everyone took off except the servant and Mr. Petrie.

The servant was confused. "What do I do now?" he asked his partner.

"Just pick up the wheelbarrow and run!"

Not knowing any better, the servant picked up the whole wheelbarrow with Mr. Petrie still in it!

Gorgool had been hiding, but following his servant the whole time. He was absolutely furious as he watched him join the race. He was supposed to have the backpack by now! Instead, the girl was wearing it, and the foolish servant had managed to carry Mr. Petrie and the wheelbarrow all the way to the finish line.

"The winner is ... Petrie and the big guy!" Dolores exclaimed.

Chapter 3

Warren left the cheering crowd behind and returned to the picnic blanket. That was when he finally saw what had happened. Every single ant in the farm had escaped.

Warren felt terrible. "How did this happen? My ants have got out!" He dropped down to his hands and knees and began searching the area for any ants that may have stuck around.

"Rosie! Ethel! Herman! Come on, guys!" he cried. "Come back!"

As Warren searched, the rest of the picnic group came back. Tracy, Susan and Mrs. Patterson began spreading out the picnic baskets and coolers of food.

"Who was that weirdo in the cheesy hat?" asked Susan.

"I don't know," replied Tracy, "but I don't think it's fair that he carried the whole wheelbarrow!"

Mr. Petrie and Dolores joined the group. Mr. Petrie cheerfully carried his trophy.

"Hi, guys," said Dolores. "Are you ready to try my potato salad?"

"You have to try mine first," said Mr. Petrie. "It's my grandma's special recipe!"

The teacher sat on the blanket and uncovered one of the picnic baskets. Reaching inside, he pulled out a huge tub of potato salad. But something was wrong. Mr. Petrie dropped the salad in a hurry and stood up. He began madly brushing himself and wiggling around in a crazy dance.

Dolores chuckled. "What's the matter, Petrie? Ants in your pants?"

That was when everyone noticed the ants. They swarmed all over the blanket now that the basket was open. Mrs. Patterson threw her sandwich away, screaming, when she noticed ants crawling through it.

Tracy shot Warren an angry look. "Warren!" she shouted at him, disgusted.

"I don't know how it happened," her brother replied. Warren looked embarrassed. Even worse, he had no idea how he'd ever get his ants back in the ant farm.

"We'd better pack up the food that's

left and go home right now," said the kids' mother. She began gathering up what little hadn't been overrun by ants.

Tracy got an idea. "Wait, mom! We've spent days organizing this picnic!"

"Well, I don't think any of us want to stick around and get eaten alive."

"Just give it a minute," said Tracy. "I know a way to make the ants go away. I promise!" The girl grabbed her backpack and took off out of sight.

Warren was suspicious. He had a hunch that Tracy was going to try one of her magic spells. That meant a 50-50 chance that something would go terribly wrong.

Quite some time ago, one of the book's spells had accidently turned Warren, while he was sneezing, into a big, blue monster. Now, every time Warren sneezed, he changed from looking like Warren, to looking like the Monster, and back again.

Ducking behind a tree nearby, Tracy pulled out the Book of Spells and the Jewel of Fenrath. "I'm sure I saw a spell to get rid of insects in here," she said, flipping through the pages of the book. "Yes! Here it is."

Tracy held up the jewel and began to chant the spell. "*Ich stem nimoy scarpatious insecta flek!*" The jewel glowed bright blue as Tracy recited the spell.

A bright, blue beam shot from the jewel heading for the picnic area. Warren saw this and followed it back to the source. Seeing his sister with the Book of Spells open, he cried out in shock. "Tracy, no!"

It was too late, though. The blue energy died down and the spell was complete.

Back at the picnic blanket, Mrs. Patterson looked around. She was amazed.

"Would you look at that? Tracy was right! The ants seem to be all gone."

Tracy's friend Susan also checked out the food. "Oh, you're right, Mrs. Patterson!"

Tracy returned to the picnic site with a big smile on her face. "See everyone? What did I tell you? Ants are no problem."

Everyone sat back down on the blanket, happy to be able to finish their lunch. They hardly noticed a rhythmic thud in the ground. Nor did they pay much attention when a dark shadow seemed to block out the sun.

"Oh no," said Susan, "it's getting cloudy. I hope it doesn't rain." She held out her hand to see if there were any rain drops falling. That was when she noticed the looks of horror on the faces of everyone else.

"What is it?" she asked. Without a word, the whole group pointed behind Susan. Slowly the girl turned around. What she saw made her jaw drop.

Looming over the girl was an ant. Not just an ordinary ant, but a real giant. It towered over everyone, clicking its mouth open and shut. Its shiny outer shell looked like armor.

Tracy jumped to her feet, knocking the Jewel of Fenrath out of her bag. Susan screamed! Mrs. Patterson cried out for help! Everyone but Warren panicked.

Warren kept his cool. He looked up at the giant ant and asked, "Is that you, Herman?"

Chapter 4

When the screaming died down, Dolores got over her fear of the giant ant. Her police officer instincts kicked in. As she kept telling the kids, she was a "highly trained police professional." She knew it was up to her to restore peace and order to the park.

"Halt in the name of the law!" Dolores shouted.

The ant, however, didn't care much about the name of the law. He decided instead to feast on what was left of the picnic, but suddenly he stopped.

Dolores smiled, thinking she was successful in halting the creature. What she didn't know was that the blue Jewel of Fenrath had caught the ant's attention. The giant ant moved its face close to the

jewel and began to make an odd purring sound.

The Patterson's aunt decided to seize the advantage. She whipped out a pair of handcuffs and approached slowly. "You're charged with creating a disturbance and attempting to eat other people's property!"

The ant continued to ignore Officer Dolores. It grabbed the jewel, then reared up on its hind legs, and took off with incredible speed. The ant crashed straight through a nearby equipment storage shed, scattering chunks of the building in its path.

Tracy approached her brother. She looked ashamed. "This is all my fault!" she cried. "I cast a spell to get rid of those ants, not make them big."

Warren was upset. "They were my pets, Tracy! That big one is Herman!"

"I'm sorry."

"Well, come on. We have to undo that spell before Herman does any more damage." The kids raced after the giant ant.

At least the ant was easy to follow. It left a trail of destruction behind it. Herman kept knocking over fences, trees and park equipment without ever slowing down.

With some effort, the Patterson kids managed to get close to the giant ant.

"I'll distract him while you reverse the spell," said Warren.

"Got it."

Warren confronted Herman. His pet ant was busy wrecking a swing set. "Herman!" he cried. "Stop!"

The ant stopped what it was doing and looked at Warren. "Good boy. It's me, Warren, okay?"

The ant tilted its head, examining the boy as if it was thinking about something.

Warren called to his sister. "Hurry, Tracy! He's not going to stay still forever!"

Tracy held the Book of Spells at the ready and reached into her bag for the jewel. That's when she really panicked!

"Warren!" she shouted. "I can't find the jewel. I must have dropped it back at the park!"

In the distance, the kids heard their mother calling for them. The ant used their confusion to take off. When Mrs. Patterson finally found her children, Herman was long gone.

"What are you kids doing out here? There's a giant ant on the loose!" she cried.

"But Mom," Warren began.

"No buts, Warren," his mom replied. "I want you two safely home. Let Aunt Dolores handle this giant ant."

Chapter 5

Herman, the giant ant, wandered down the middle of a formerly peaceful street. People ran screaming from the giant insect. But Herman was not out to cause destruction. In truth, he was a very gentle ant. It's just that he couldn't control his very large body – and he was hungry!

Herman followed a trail of potato salad blobs, trying to get a little lunch. The food trail led away from the busy areas of town and off to the ruins of the old Amberson mansion.

Purely by accident, Herman had stumbled on Gorgool's hideout. The evil creature and his servant were down in the basement, and Gorgool was busy shouting at him.

"You simpleton! You were supposed to steal the backpack, not a picnic basket!"

The servant was grinning foolishly. "Sorry, master, but the potato salad was so yummy. And look, I got a trophy for winning the race!" He held up a small gold-plated statue of a wheelbarrow.

They heard a noise scratching at the door which led outside.

"Did you hear something, master?"

"No! And don't change the subject! I'm not finished scolding you yet!"

Actually, Gorgool's scolding ended in seconds. Herman burst through the door leading to the basement lair. The scent of potato salad was in the air, and the hungry ant was determined to find more of it.

Gorgool spun around, furious at the intrusion.

"Who dares enter without knocking?" he demanded. Suddenly a look of wonder crossed the evil fiend's face as he looked up at the giant ant.

Herman, on the other hand, went straight for the potato salad. Before he could gorge himself, he turned his head and spat out something shiny and blue.

Gorgool couldn't believe his eyes. "The Jewel of Fenrath!" he cried with

glee. "Quickly, servant! Take the jewel before this thing tries to get it back!"

"But master…"

"Are you disobeying my command!" shrieked Gorgool.

The servant gulped. "No, mighty Gorgool."

Gorgool's man slowly approached the giant ant and the jewel.

Herman had finished the potato salad in no time flat and picked up the Jewel of Fenrath just as the servant grabbed for it. Having no other choice, he closed his eyes and reached into the mouth of the insect.

"Please, please don't bite me!" the servant begged. Quickly he plucked out the jewel and put it into his pocket.

Gorgool kept staring at the ant, absorbed by the creature. "That's right," he said. "Let him have the jewel. That's a good boy, now sit!"

Herman slowly sat down. The servant also sat down on the floor.

"Not you, you fool! Just the ant! Now, lie down."

The ant obeyed and lay down on the floor with no protest. The servant once again followed the order.

"I'm still just talking to the ant, you imbecile! Go away!"

The servant got to his feet. "Good idea, master. He's scary! Make him go away right now!"

"That time I *was* talking to you!" shouted Gorgool.

"You mean, you don't want the ant to go away?" asked the servant, confused.

"Certainly not!" Gorgool walked towards Herman, making his round prison roll with him. The giant insect had rolled to its back like some strange puppy dog. "This wonderful creature has brought me the jewel. I'm going to keep it as my pet!"

"It's a funny-looking pet, master," replied the servant.

Gorgool ignored him. "We must give it a name, though." Gorgool thought for a moment, stroking his pointed chin. "Ah, yes. We'll call him Maltar!"

The servant looked at the giant ant with wide eyes. "Maltar?"

"Indeed," said the fiend. "This ant will bring me my freedom – which is more than you've ever managed to do."

Chapter 6

Officer Dolores was riding her motorcycle around the Pickford streets. With that giant ant on the loose, she called for the streets to be evacuated. Everyone had to be in their houses until the ant was found. Many of the residents of the town were so afraid, they had boarded up their windows and doors.

With a screech, Dolores stopped her motorcycle out front of the Patterson's house. She honked the horn on the bike and Mrs. Patterson carefully opened the door to the house. She was relieved to see her sister-in-law and not a giant ant attacking.

"What is it, Dolores?" she asked. Tracy and Warren joined their mother at the door. Their Aunt pulled out a truly horrible pencil sketch of the giant ant.

"Take a look at Pickford's Public Enemy Number One!"

Warren was horrified. That didn't look like Herman one bit!

"Pretty good likeness, eh?" said Dolores. "I drew the mutant myself, all

from memory." She seemed very proud of her work.

"What are you going to do if you catch him?" asked Tracy.

"You won't hurt him, will you?" asked a worried Warren.

Dolores gave Warren a look. "Hey, kiddo, whose side are you on?"

Mrs. Patterson interrupted. "We're on your side, of course, Dolores. Now kids, nobody leaves this house until that thing is caught. Is that clear?" She gave her children a look of warning that only a mother can give.

Tracy and Warren stared down at their feet. "Yes, Mom," they replied together, disappointed that they now couldn't search for the missing Jewel of Fenrath.

"Well, duty calls," said Dolores buckling her motorcycle helmet. "I gotta go find me a bug expert to see about tracking this guy down."

"You could ask Mr. Petrie," suggested Warren. "He knows all about ants."

"Petrie, eh? We'll have to see about that."

*   *   *

Back in Gorgool's basement hideout, the evil ruler was giving yet more orders to his bumbling servant. The servant himself was holding a dog leash and staring down at it.

"Take Maltar for a walk," said Gorgool. "He needs some exercise before I send him out to get the book."

"Yes, master," said the sad and reluctant servant.

"And keep him on that leash. Whatever you do, don't let him out of your sight for a second!"

*   *   *

Stuck in their own house, Warren and Tracy decided to get some advice from Johnny the Ghost. They burst into the attic just as Johnny was about to play his trumpet. Startled, he choked into the mouthpiece and made a funny tooting noise.

"Johnny!" shouted the kids.

The ghost set his trumpet down and turned to the Patterson kids. "Oh, that was a bad B-flat. But what's cooking? Have you found the jewel yet?"

"No," said Warren. "We need you to do us a favor."

"What can I do for you?" asked the ghost.

"Well you know we're not allowed outside right now," started Tracy, "so we wondered if you could fly over Pickford for us. See if you can spot Herman anywhere on the ground."

Johnny gave the kids a crisp, military

salute and winked. "Okey dokey, cap-
tain!" The ghost disappeared through
the roof of the house in search of the
giant ant.

*   *   *

Johnny was getting frustrated after covering much of the town. Nothing was happening at all. All the townspeople were indoors, and there was no sign of the giant ant outdoors.

"Where could that ant have gone?" Johnny asked himself. "Maybe he left Pickford."

The ghost turned back towards the Patterson's home. On his way back he passed over the area where he knew Gorgool and his servant had their hideout. That was when he spotted movement. Down below was Gorgool's servant – walking a giant ant on a leash.

"Holy horn section!" cried the ghost. "Gorgool has turned the ant into his pet!"

Chapter 7

The servant continued to walk "Maltar" in a circle around the debris in the area. He kept shooting the ant dirty looks as they walked.

"Whatever you do, don't let him out of your sight for a second…" muttered the servant making fun of Gorgool's voice. "Gorgool must like you better than me now," he said to the ant.

The ant responded with an odd purring noise. Herman could not have known that the servant would be jealous.

Suddenly the slow-witted servant got a sly look on his face. He paused to look around, making sure no one could see. Then he unfastened the leash from the giant ant.

"Go on, get out of here!" the servant

shouted at Gorgool's pet. "Run away! Shoo!" He waved his hands at the ant, trying to get rid of him as best he could.

Herman wasn't sure what the servant wanted, but he tried his best to keep him happy. If that meant turning and walking away, that's just what he would do.

*   *   *

Back at Pickford Elementary School, Dolores found Mr. Petrie in the school's science lab. Taking Warren's advice, she approached the teacher and asked for a lesson on ants. Mr. Petrie pulled down a chart to begin a quick lecture.

"Okay Professor," said Dolores, sitting at a desk as if she were a regular student, "tell me all I need to know about these critters. I need to collar this mutant ASAP." She pulled out a notebook and pen to write down important information.

"Well, they're strong," Mr. Petrie began. "Very strong. A normal ant can lift many times its own weight. So a giant ant would have enormous strength."

Dolores was scribbling in her notebook furiously.

"Ants are very industrious. They dig

vast networks of tunnels under the ground."

"What else?" Dolores asked.

"Oh! Ants are very smart. They have the biggest brain compared to the size of their body of any insect."

Dolores looked up from her writing. "Brains, shmains. It's up against me,

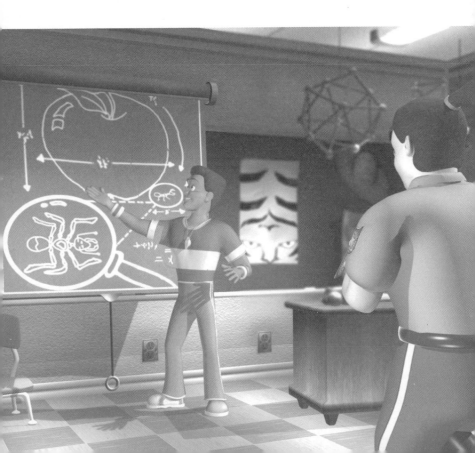

remember? Wherever it is, I'll catch it!"

Neither of them noticed the face in the classroom window. It was Herman — peeking in at them! The giant ant seemed to be laughing at Aunt Dolores.

Mr. Petrie stroked his chin thoughtfully. "I just got an idea on how you might catch it, Dolores. A giant, sticky pest strip! Once the ant steps on it, he'd be as good as caught."

"Where can we find something like that?" she asked.

"We'll build one here in the school, right here in the science lab."

*   *   *

The servant returned to the basement hideout after getting rid of the pesky ant. As he entered the lair, Gorgool spun around to face him.

"What took so long!" he shouted.

Gorgool was always impatient. "I was beginning to worry . . . wait! Where's Maltar?" he snapped, sounding very evil indeed.

"He, uh, accidentally escaped and ran away," lied the servant.

Gorgool gulped loudly. "You lost Maltar?"

The servant thought he should try to cheer up his boss. "I tried to stop him, Gorgool, but he wouldn't obey me. Then he tried to bite me."

"Bite you?"

"Yes, master. He pulled and yanked and ... and I just couldn't stop him."

The servant was afraid Gorgool would be very angry. But suddenly Gorgool's evil glare changed to a smile. "Maltar!" he cried.

The servant, confused, turned around. While he was talking, the giant insect had returned and stood behind him.

Gorgool had a strangely love-struck look on his face. "He missed me," he said, "and now he's come home."

Then he turned angrily to the servant. "Now, show him the drawing, you fool! This ant will set me free!"

Chapter 8

The servant picked up a crude drawing he had made earlier. It was a picture of the one thing that Gorgool still desired – the Book of Spells in Tracy's backpack.

"See, Maltar?" said Gorgool. "That book inside the bag? I want you to get me

that book. Bring it to Grover's Field where the picnic was. Understand?"

The ant nodded once and Gorgool smiled.

"Now fetch the book, my beauty. Fetch!"

Just like a happy puppy, the giant ant took off from the basement lair in search of its prize. It didn't have to go far.

Tracy and Warren were minutes away from the entrance to Gorgool's hideout at the Amberson place. When Johnny told them that the evil fiend had the ant, the kids made a quick plan to sneak outside. Johnny stayed in Warren's room playing his trumpet – something that Warren also did. Tracy was supposedly listening to "Warren" practice, but the kids slipped out the window instead.

"There's Herman!" cried Warren, spotting his pet. "Herman!"

The ant started right for the kids. More accurately, it started right for Tracy's backpack. When the creature reached them, it immediately grabbed the bag in its mouth. Tracy was far too small to fight back.

"Hey, you, that's mine! Give it back!" shouted Tracy.

Warren tried to calm the situation down. "There's just a book in that backpack, Herman," he said using his pet's original name. "It's nothing you'd want."

Tracy thought for a split second. "Unless Gorgool's already got the jewel and Herman is following his orders!"

The ant nodded, understanding them perfectly. Warren and Tracy shared a horrified look.

"We'd better let the Monster handle this, sis," suggested Warren. He picked a dandelion that was growing nearby and sniffed it deeply. Warren was allergic to just about everything and sneezed noisily.

Warren's sneeze turned him into the large blue monster. Warren glowed brightly and was surrounded by zaps of power. He grew and grew, his skin turning a rather nice shade of blue, getting tough and leathery. In moments, he turned into the Monster!

Now he had more than enough strength and size to tackle the giant ant. Jumping at the giant insect, the Monster

grabbed for the backpack. Gaining a hold, the two creatures began a mighty tug-of-war.

The Monster knew he wasn't getting anywhere against the ant this way. Since he was a good deal bigger than even a giant ant, he shoved back in the other direction. The Monster pinned the ant against a tree.

"You gonna say 'uncle' now?" he asked.

The ant dropped the bag, defeated. The Monster bent and picked it up. He turned back to his sister and took one step towards her when something strange happened. A sudden stroke of blue lightning sizzled over the ant. Suddenly Herman shuddered and grew even bigger. He became the same size as the Monster!

"Oh my gosh!" cried Tracy, looking up at the towering bug.

When the Monster turned back to his pet, his jaw dropped. Unfortunately, so did Tracy's backpack. The giant ant took that moment to grab the backpack and run away into the nearby street.

Tracy turned to her brother. "Quick! Before he gets away with the book."

The girl and the Monster took off after the ant. Herman tried to escape by dodging down an alleyway.

"He just went in there," indicated the Monster. "There's no way he can escape!"

The pair rounded the corner just moments after their prey. Then they stopped dead and moaned in despair at what they saw.

The ant had burrowed deep into the ground. Tracy's empty backpack lay on the ground beside the freshly dug tunnel.

Chapter 9

Tracy and the Monster stared into the dark opening of the tunnel. The hole seemed to lead deep underground. Given his giant size, Herman might have dug down for miles.

Tracy slammed a fist into her palm. "Herman is taking the book straight to Gorgool. I know it!"

"What do we do now?" asked the Monster.

The girl looked up at her brother. A daring look crossed her face and the Monster tensed. He knew that look well – and it always led to trouble.

In one quick movement, Tracy stepped forward and leapt into the hole.

The Monster stared down the tunnel, shocked. "Tracy?" he called. There was no

reply. Nervous now, he called again. "Are you alright? Can you hear me?"

Tracy's voice echoed out of the hole. "I'm fine! Come on, we have to catch that ant!"

The Monster, relieved that his sister was safe, hopped into the dark tunnel...

*   *   *

At the moment Tracy and the Monster leapt into the unknown, Dolores and Mr. Petrie walked from the school. Together, they carried a giant pest strip with them. It was so big they kept stumbling with it, almost sticking to it themselves.

Mr. Petrie stumbled. He was carrying the back end. "Ugh! Where are we taking this thing, anyway?"

Since Dolores was in front, she was in charge of steering the pest strip. "Grover's Field," she said.

"Why there?"

"Don't you know that the criminal always returns to the scene of the crime?"

Mr. Petrie just rolled his eyes.

Back in the ant's tunnel, Tracy led the Monster beneath the streets of Pickford. They could faintly hear the creature digging up ahead of them. It was too dark to move fast enough to catch up, though.

"Do you see anything?" asked Tracy.

The Monster shook his head, then realized Tracy couldn't see him. "No. I don't even see a light at the end of this tunnel."

"At least Herman is making some noise," said Tracy. "We know we're going in the right direction."

That was when the noise stopped. In its place a very faint glow appeared.

"Look!" said Tracy. "He must have gone back up to the surface."

"We'd better hurry, then," said a grim Monster. "And be careful, Tracy. Gorgool will be waiting at the end of this tunnel."

*   *   *

The ant came up right in the middle of Grover's Field, where this whole mess began. Herman could see his master a little ways off waiting with the servant. Approaching Gorgool, the ant dropped his prize in front of his new master. It was, of course, the Book of Spells.

Gorgool would have drooled over it if he hadn't been trapped inside his ball. Instead, he gleefully rubbed his hands together. "At last! I have the Book of Spells and the Jewel of Fenrath together! I can finally be rid of this prison! Good work, Maltar." The evil one turned to his servant. "Do you still have that trophy of yours?"

The servant eagerly pulled his wheelbarrow prize from a pocket. "Here! You want to see it again?"

"No, you fool. Give it to Maltar as a reward."

The servant was shocked. "But . . . master . . ." he began.

"Now!" shouted Gorgool.

The servant held back a sniffle as he took one last look at his trophy. Turning to the ant, he held out the prize. With two quick chomps, the hungry ant had eaten the poor servant's trophy.

"Now," said Gorgool, "take out the jewel and read the spell that will free me!"

Holding the book open, the servant began to read. "*Ich fenoom bar grishnak . . .*" A wind began to blow through the park. The jewel began to glow. "*Pon stemoy flang kratoff spleen . . .*" The servant had almost finished when the book went flying from his hands.

The Monster had burst in – just in time!

"Nice job," Tracy commented.

"The pleasure was all mine," the Monster told her.

But Gorgool was beside himself with anger. "Don't let that blue ape stop you!

The spell is almost complete!" he cried.

As the servant bent to pick up the book, the Monster pushed him aside. The book itself was sent flying into Tracy's capable hands.

"I'll take over from here!" she shouted triumphantly.

The wind was continuing to blow. Even with the spell unfinished, the magic still had some effect.

Gorgool was furious. "Maltar! Get that girl!"

"Not if I can help it," said the Monster.

The giant ant and the Monster, equal in size and strength, grappled with each other. The Monster would have won, too, if the wind hadn't blown a nose-ful of dust right in his face.

"Ah-ah-choo."

The dust made the Monster sneeze. And sneezing turned him back into little Warren Patterson.

"Uh-oh," said the regular-sized Warren.

Just to add to the confusion, the kids' aunt Dolores and Mr. Petrie arrived with their homemade ant trap.

"Stand back, kids! Your Aunt is coming to save you!" cried the police officer.

A strong gust of wind lifted the giant pest strip off the ground. The cop and the

teacher tried their best to control it, but it flipped, twisted and landed at their feet. Dolores and Mr. Petrie tripped, landing face first and stuck in their own trap.

Tracy used the distraction to grab the Jewel of Fenrath. The giant ant saw what she was up to. Moving quickly, it grabbed the jewel in its mouth. Shaking the jewel, the ant nearly doubled in size. The magic created by shaking the jewel made Herman grow larger and larger.

"Herman, no!" cried Warren. "Give me the jewel and I'll give you a treat later!"

Gorgool wasn't going to back down yet. "Don't listen to that brat, Maltar!"

"Herman, please!" called Warren.

"Maltar!" screamed Gorgool.

The ant looked confused. Whether by accident or not, he swallowed the jewel. He lay down on the ground as if he had a stomach ache!

Tracy seized the moment. Flipping open the Book of Spells, she began to read. "*Ich stem nimoy scarpatious insecta flek...*"

He's got the jewel inside him!" cried Gorgool.

Tracy kept on. "*Stementa bursatola...*"

"He's got my trophy!" shouted the servant.

Tracy continued. "*Gargola stanta sek.*"

"Don't hurt him, Tracy!" warned Warren.

Tracy gritted her teeth and did what she had to. "*Bricken blaxen!*"

Herman, the giant ant began to glow bright blue. Finally the blue light grew so bright that everyone had to cover their eyes.

Chapter 10

When the flash of light was finished, everyone looked around. The ant appeared to be gone, but everything it had eaten was lying in the grass – including the jewel and the servant's trophy.

The wind died down and Tracy scooped up the jewel. "That was some spell reversal!" she said.

Warren was on his hands and knees, searching the ground, when he spotted something small and black. "Herman!" he cried, lifting the ant with his finger.

Gorgool looked forlorn. He'd lost his chance at escape and his only pet. "Maltar," he moaned. "You took away my Maltar."

"You still have me, Gorgool," said the servant, loyal to the end.

Gorgool stared at his servant. Opening his mouth, he let out a huge, angry roar. The servant wisely picked him up and ran for the safety of the Amberson mansion hideout.

The kids, job done, began to head for home. Warren looked back down at his

pet. "I'm going to have to get Herman a whole bunch of new friends now."

Tracy smiled at her brother. "I don't think he could ever have one as loyal as you, Warren."

Warren stopped suddenly, staring at a nearby tree.

"What is it?" asked Tracy.

Ahead of the kids were Dolores and Mr. Petrie, still stuck to the ant trap. The kids had been so busy with the ant and Gorgool that they didn't even notice the two of them. Nor had Dolores and Petrie seen the Monster change into Warren.

"This is all your fault, Petrie!" came Dolores' muffled shout.

"Oh yeah?" he retorted. "Well, you're the one in charge, remember?"

The Patterson kids could hardly believe the situation these adults got themselves into.

"Good thing we got to Herman first, right Tracy?" Warren told his sister.

Tracy began to crack a smile, trying not to laugh. "He would never have stood a chance against . . ."

The brother and sister shared a look. Then both of them blurted out ". . . a highly trained police professional!"

The End

About the people who brought you this book

Located in Toronto, Canada, **CCI Entertainment** has been producing quality family entertainment since 1982. Some of their best known shows are "Sharon Lois and Bram's The Elephant Show," "Eric's World," and of course, "Monster By Mistake"!

Catapult Productions in Toronto wants to entertain the whole world with computer animation. Now that we've entertained you, there are only 5 billion people to go!

Mark Mayerson grew up loving animated cartoons and now has a job making them. "Monster By Mistake" is the first TV show he created.

Paul Kropp is an author, editor and educator. His work includes young adult novels, novels for reluctant readers, and the bestselling *How to Make Your Child a Reader for Life*.

MONSTER By Mistake! Videos

Six Monster By Mistake home videos are available and more are on the way.

Each video contains 2 episodes and comes with a special Monster surprise!

Only $9.99 each.

Monster By Mistake & Entertaining Orville
1-55366-130-3

Fossel Remains & Kidnapped 1-55366-131-1

Monster a Go-Go & Home Alone 1-55366-132-X

Billy Caves In & Tracy's Jacket 1-55366-202-4

Campsite Creeper & Johnny's Reunion
1-55366-201-6

Gorgool's Pet & Jungle Land
1-55366-200-8

TOP SECRET!

Sneak Preview of New
Monster By Mistake Episodes

Even more all-new monster-iffic episodes of Monster By Mistake are on the way in 2003 and 2004! Here's an inside look at what's ahead for Warren, Tracy and Johnny:

- It promises to be a battle royale when a superstar wrestler comes to town and challenges the Monster to a match at the Pickford arena.

- There's a gorilla on the loose in Pickford, but where did it come from? It's up to the Monster, Tracy and Johnny to catch the gorilla and solve the mystery.

- When making deliveries for a bakery, Warren discovers who robbed the Pickford Savings and Loan. Can the Monster stop the robbers from getting away?

- Warren, Tracy and Johnny visit Fenrath, the home to Gorgool, the Book of Spells and the jewel. In Fenrath, they discover who imprisoned Gorgool in the ball and what they must do to restore order to this magical kingdom.

Visit the amazing
award-winning

MONSTER
By Mistake!

website

www.monsterbymistake.com

- ❏ experience a 3-D on line adventure
- ❏ preview the next episodes
- ❏ play lots of cool games
- ❏ join the international fan club (it's free)
- ❏ test your knowledge with the trivia quiz
- ❏ visit a full library of audio and video clips
- ❏ enter exciting contests to win GREAT PRIZES
- ❏ surf in English or French